This Ladybird Book belongs to:

_____

_____

_____

_____

This Ladybird retelling
by
Nicola Baxter

Ladybird books are widely available, but in case of
difficulty may be ordered by post or telephone from:

Ladybird Books – Cash Sales Department
Littlegate Road Paignton Devon TQ3 3BE
Telephone 01803 554761

A catalogue record for this book is available
from the British Library

Published by Ladybird Books Ltd Loughborough Leicestershire UK
Ladybird Books Inc Auburn Maine 04210 USA

© LADYBIRD BOOKS LTD 1993

LADYBIRD and the device of a Ladybird are trademarks of Ladybird Books Ltd
All rights reserved. No part of this publication may be reproduced,
stored in a retrieval system, or transmitted in any form or by any
means, electronic, mechanical, photocopying, recording or otherwise,
without the prior consent of the copyright owner.

FAVOURITE TALES

Little Red Riding Hood

*illustrated
by
PETER STEVENSON*

based on the story by Jacob and Wilhelm Grimm

Once upon a time there was a little girl who loved to visit her grandmother. The old woman was always busy making something for her favourite granddaughter.

One day she made something very special indeed. It was a beautiful, bright red cape with a hood. The little girl loved it so much that she wore it all the time!

Soon everyone started calling her "Little Red Riding Hood".

One morning the little girl's mother said, "Little Red Riding Hood, your grandmother is not very well. I am packing up some things to help her feel better and I'd like you to take them to her.

"But *do* be careful as you walk through the forest. And *don't* stop for anything on the way!"

"I'll be *very* careful," promised Little Red Riding Hood, "and I won't stop for a second."

So off she went with her little basket. She waved to her mother until she was out of sight.

Just at the edge of the forest, a very crafty fellow was waiting.

It was a wolf! When Little Red Riding Hood passed by, he greeted her with a slow smile.

"Good morning, my dear," he said. "And what a fine morning it is!"

Little Red Riding Hood had never met a wolf before, so she wasn't scared. "Good morning," she said politely, "but I'm afraid I can't stop and talk."

"No matter, my dear," said the wolf. "I shall walk along with you. Where are you off to, this fine morning?"

"I'm going to see my grandmother," replied Little Red Riding Hood.

"Then I think I can be of service," said the wolf. "I'll show you where there are some lovely flowers, my dear. You can take her a bouquet."

Little Red Riding Hood knew that she shouldn't stop, but she did like the idea of taking her grandmother a special present. So she followed the wolf.

"Here we are," he said. "Now I must fly. I am late for my lunch."

When Little Red Riding Hood reached her grandmother's house, she was a little bit surprised to see that the door was open.

"Is that you, my dear?" croaked a faint voice. "Do come in!"

But when Little Red Riding Hood crept up to her grandmother's bed, a very strange sight met her eyes.

"Oh, Grandmother!" she cried. "What big ears you have!"

"All the better to hear you with, my dear," came the reply.

Little Red Riding Hood went a little closer.

"Oh, Grandmother! What big eyes you have!" she gasped.

"All the better to see you with, my dear!"

Little Red Riding Hood took one more step.

"Oh, Grandmother! What big teeth you have!"

"All the better to eat you with!" cried the wolf, and he gobbled her up!

When Little Red Riding Hood did not come home that afternoon, her parents were very worried. At last her father went to Grandmother's cottage to find her.

How horrified he was when he found a fierce animal in Grandmother's bed! With one blow of his axe, he killed the wicked wolf.

Then Little Red Riding Hood's father carefully cut open the wolf. Out jumped the little girl! She felt very strange indeed.

"Where is Grandmother?" she asked.

"I'm in here!" cried a muffled voice from inside the wolf. Little Red Riding Hood and her father soon pulled the old lady out and tucked her up in bed.

"I feel a lot better now!" said Little Red Riding Hood's grandmother, as she tasted the good things the little girl had brought.

Little Red Riding Hood's mother was so glad her little girl was safe that she hadn't the heart to scold her.

"I know you won't stop to pick flowers next time, Little Red Riding Hood," she said, "because *I* will give you some to take to Grandmother!"